The Frog Prince and the Kitten

by Clare De Marco

Illustrated by Alison Edgson

W
FRANKLIN WATTS
LONDON • SYDNEY

First published in 2013 by
Franklin Watts
338 Euston Road
London
NW1 3BH

Franklin Watts Australia
Level 17/207 Kent Street
Sydney
NSW 2000

A CIP catalogue record for this book is available
from the British Library.

ISBN 978 1 4451 1614 3 (hbk)
ISBN 978 1 4451 1620 4 (pbk)

Series Editor: Jackie Hamley
Series Advisor: Catherine Glavina
Series Designer: Peter Scoulding

Printed in China

Franklin Watts is a divison of
Hachette Children's Books,
an Hachette UK company.
www.hachette.co.uk

Once upon a time, a
kitten called Lily lived
outside a beautiful palace.

She loved chasing the mice
and the birds.

The mice and the birds
did not like being chased
at all.

But Lily loved scaring
them as she zoomed
around the garden.

She was a menace.

One day, Lily found
a golden ball.

She knocked it with
her paws.

Then the ball went
SPLASH and fell
down a well.

Just as Lily was
peering down the well,
a little frog appeared.

15

"I will get your ball!" croaked the frog. "If you promise not to chase the other animals."

Lily loved that ball.
"All right," she agreed.

The frog disappeared,
and soon returned with
the ball.

Lily watched the frog hop towards her.

It was just too much.

She started to chase him.

With a giant leap, Lily pounced on the frog.

As she did, something odd happened.

Lily was sitting on top of
a large dog.

"I'm Prince," barked the dog. "A witch put a spell on me for chasing her cat.

It could only be broken by
a kitten's touch!"

"Now I'm a dog again," barked Prince, "I can CHASE YOU!"

28

Puzzle 1

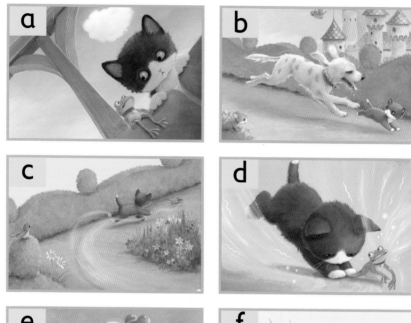

Put these pictures in the correct order.
Now tell the story in your own words.
How short can you make the story?

Puzzle 2

cheeky   naughty

miserable

annoyed   tired

cross

Choose the words which best describe the characters. Can you think of any more? Pretend to be one of the characters!

Answers

Puzzle 1

The correct order is:

1c, 2a, 3e, 4d, 5f, 6b

Puzzle 2

Lily　　The correct words are cheeky, naughty.

　　　　　The incorrect word is miserable.

Mice　　The correct words are annoyed, cross.

　　　　　The incorrect word is tired.

For details of all our titles go to: www.franklinwatts.co.uk

*hardback